Dear Parent:
Your child's love of reading starts here!

Every child learns to read in a different way and at his or her own speed. Some go back and forth between reading levels and read favorite books again and again. Others read through each level in order. You can help your young reader improve and become more confident by encouraging his or her own interests and abilities. From books your child reads with you to the first books he or she reads alone, there are I Can Read Books for every stage of reading:

SHARED READING
Basic language, word repetition, and whimsical illustrations, ideal for sharing with your emergent reader

BEGINNING READING
Short sentences, familiar words, and simple concepts for children eager to read on their own

READING WITH HELP
Engaging stories, longer sentences, and language play for developing readers

READING ALONE
Complex plots, challenging vocabulary, and high-interest topics for the independent reader

ADVANCED READING
Short paragraphs, chapters, and exciting themes for the perfect bridge to chapter books

I Can Read Books have introduced children to the joy of reading since 1957. Featuring award-winning authors and illustrators and a fabulous cast of beloved characters, I Can Read Books set the standard for beginning readers.

A lifetime of discovery begins with the magical words **"I Can Read!"**

Visit www.icanread.com for information
on enriching your child's reading experience.

I Can Read Book® is a trademark of HarperCollins Publishers.

Pete the Kitty and the Case of the Hiccups
Copyright © 2019 by James Dean
Pete the Cat is a registered trademark of Pete the Cat, LLC.
All rights reserved. Printed in the United States of America.
No part of this book may be used or reproduced in any manner whatsoever without written permission except in the case of
brief quotations embodied in critical articles and reviews. For information address HarperCollins Children's Books, a division of
HarperCollins Publishers, 195 Broadway, New York, NY 10007.
www.icanread.com

Library of Congress Control Number: 2018947890
ISBN 978-0-06-286827-5 (trade bdg.) — ISBN 978-0-06-286826-8 (pbk.)

The artist used pen and ink, with watercolor and acrylic paint on 300lb hot press paper to create the illustrations for this book.

18 19 20 21 22 LSCC 10 9 8 7 6 5 4 3 2 1 ❖ First Edition

I Can Read!

SHARED
My First
READING

Pete the Kitty
AND THE CASE OF THE
HICCUPS

HIC!

by James Dean

HARPER
An Imprint of HarperCollinsPublishers

"Hiccup!"

Oh no!

Pete has the hiccups!

"Hiccup! Hiccup!"

How do you stop the hiccups?

Pete asks Grumpy Toad,
"How do I stop my hiccups?"

"I know!" says Grumpy Toad.
"You stand on one foot."

Pete stands on one foot.
"Hiccup!"

Pete still has the hiccups.

Pete asks Callie,

"How do I stop my hiccups?"

"I know!" says Callie.
"You stand on one foot
and hop up and down."

11

Pete stands on one foot.

He hops up and down.

"Hiccup! Hiccup!"

Pete still has the hiccups.

Pete asks Gus,

"How do I stop my hiccups?"

"I know!" says Gus.

"You stand on one foot
and hop up and down
and sing a song."

15

Pete stands on one foot.

He hops up and down.

He sings a song.

"Hiccup! Hiccup! Hiccup!"
Pete still has the hiccups.

Pete asks Bob,

"How do I stop my hiccups?"

18

"I know!" says Bob.

"You stand on one foot
and hop up and down
and sing a song
and rub your belly!"
says Bob.

Pete does it.

HIC!

"Hiccup!"

Nothing is working!

Pete still has the hiccups.

"Go ask Mom," says Bob.

Pete asks Mom,
"How do I stop my hiccups?"
"I know!" says Mom.

"You take a deep breath."

Pete takes a deep breath.

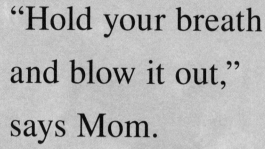

"Hold your breath
and blow it out,"
says Mom.

Pete holds his breath.

Pete blows his breath out.

"That's it?" Pete asks.

"That's it!" says Mom.

Pete waits.

And he waits.

And he waits.

The hiccups are gone!

Moms are so smart!

32